Brander Matthews

The Decision of the Court

A comedy

Brander Matthews

The Decision of the Court
A comedy

ISBN/EAN: 9783744781534

Printed in Europe, USA, Canada, Australia, Japan

Cover: Foto ©Andreas Hilbeck / pixelio.de

More available books at **www.hansebooks.com**

MR. BRANDER MATTHEWS

THE DECISION OF THE COURT

A Comedy

BY

BRANDER MATTHEWS

ILLUSTRATED

NEW YORK

HARPER & BROTHERS PUBLISHERS

1893

NOTE

[This comedy was first acted in America by the Theatre of Arts and Letters at its fourth subscription performance in New York, March 23, 1893, with Mrs. Agnes Booth-Schoeffel and Mr. J. H. Gilmour as Mrs. and Mr. Stanyhurst. A performance for copyright purposes was given in London, at the Comedy Theatre, March 20th. Stage-right and copyright are therefore fully protected, both in Great Britain and in the United States.]

LIST OF ILLUSTRATIONS

THE DECISION OF THE COURT

CAST OF CHARACTERS

Mrs. ALGERNON STANYHURST.

Mr. ALGERNON STANYHURST.

THE MAID.

THE MESSENGER-BOY.

SCENE:—The parlor of Mrs. Stanyhurst's cottage at Newport, R. I.

TIME:—Late in September.

THE time is late September, and the scene is the parlor of a cottage at Newport, the broad windows of which overlook the harbor. It is a handsomely furnished room, showing that its occupant is a woman of taste. On one side there is a conservatory bow-window filled with flowers, and having a hanging bird-cage in the centre. On the other side there is a mantel-piece, with a mirror over it and a clock upon it. An open piano stands against the wall near the mantel-piece. There is a sofa near the centre of the room, with an umbrella lamp behind it.

Mrs. Stanyhurst is seen seated at a desk near the sofa engaged in writing.

Mary, the maid, enters through the draped doorway which connects the parlor and the

2

hall of the house. She stands silently behind Mrs. Stanyhurst.

Mrs. S. (*looking up*): "Well, Mary, what is it?"

Mary: "What time is it you want the tea, ma'am?"

Mrs. S.: "At five o'clock always; you will understand your duties in a day or two. And serve it promptly, whether I am here or not."

Mary (*going*): "Yes, ma'am."

Mrs. S.: "And tell Martha to have the toasted crackers hotter than they were yesterday."

Mary: "Yes, ma'am."   [*Exit.*

Mrs. S.: "Where was I? [*Taking up letter from desk and reading it aloud.*] 'If you *will* go to Japan and to India, you must not expect to have the latest news. Yes, it is true that I am suing for a divorce. Algernon and I are absolutely incompatible. If baby had lived, perhaps we might have got along together somehow—I don't know. As it was, we quarrelled every week of our second year, and almost every day of the third; yet when I try to remember what we quarrelled about, I simply can't. Algernon was disagreeable enough to say that I was the most exasperating woman he had ever met! So you see what a bad temper he has! And he was absurdly jealous ; and at the same time he was so indifferent and easy - going that he was absolutely impossible! At last

we agreed to disagree once for all, and to be
divorced. So I have been living here in
Newport for a year now all by myself—it
appears that residence is necessary—and I
have sued for divorce on the ground of non-
support. I suppose you will smile at this,
since you know my income is quite as large
as Algernon's. But that's the excuse I must
give, so my lawyer says. I have an excel-
lent lawyer, Mr. Richard Hitchcock, really
a most agreeable man, who has taken charge
of my case himself ; and he has been just
too lovely. I wish Algernon's lawyer had
been as considerate ; but his name is Bull,
and he is a brute.' [*Spoken.*] I remember
what I was going to say. [*Writing.*] 'The
case came up last week, and I testified that
Algernon hadn't given me any money for
months, and that he had abandoned me and
left the country. Algernon's lawyer made
a cheap joke about my being a grass-widow
now, and being able to make hay while the
sun shines. It's just like him to hire such

a man! The judge asked me a few questions, and then he took the papers and said he would think about it. Mr. Hitchcock tells me that we must win, of course. He hopes for a decision soon—maybe this week. He is to telegraph me at once. So perhaps before this letter gets to Chicago I shall have been unmarried.'

> [*She reads over last few lines to herself, and then signs and folds the letter.*
>
> [*While she is doing this, Mr. Stanyhurst is seen to pass the windows and to stand before door, where he rings bell.*
>
> [Mrs. Stanyhurst, *intent on folding letter and on addressing envelope, does not hear the bell. The door is opened, and* Mr. S. *disappears from view; the door closes with a bang.*

Mrs. S. (*Starting*): "Perhaps that's the decision now! Really, it is a great strain on one's nerves not to know whether one is married or not."

> [Mary *enters with card on salver.*

Mrs. S. (*Rising*): "Is it a telegram?"

Mary (*handing card*): "No, ma'am; it's a gentleman to see you."

Mrs. S. (*reading card; aside*): "Algernon! [*Surprised.*] What does he want with me?"

Mary: "He didn't say, ma'am."

Mrs. S.: "Well, you may show him in."

Mary (*going*): "Yes, ma'am."

Mrs. S.: "Stop! [*Rushes over to the mirror over the mantel-piece.*] I suppose I must look like a fright. [*Going.*] Show him in here, and say Mrs. Stanyhurst will be down in a minute."

> [*Exit through small door opposite the mantel-piece.*

MRS. AGNES BOOTH-SCHOEFFEL

Mary: "Yes, ma'am. [*Going out, and re-appearing at once with* Mr. S.] Mrs. Stanyhurst will be down in a minute, sir."

Mr. S. (*constrained and awkward*): "Certainly, certainly; there's no hurry at all-[*Seeing* Mary *waiting, he takes seat on sofa, holding hat in one hand and stick in the other.* Mary *exit.*] Really, you know, this is awkward. A man doesn't really know what to do when he has to call on his own wife, not knowing whether she is his wife or not. It is deuced awkward; that's what I call it—deuced awkward. That American judge may have given his decision to-day, you know, and when I'm talking to my wife perhaps she won't be my wife. And it was quite awkward enough before. Still, it had to be done. Wife or no wife, I wouldn't have her think I could do a thing like that, you know. [*Pause.*] She said she'd be down in a minute; but I know how long her minutes are. I suppose she's prinking before the glass. Fancy her prinking for me now! [*Pause.*] It's here she's been living since I abandoned her, as we agreed when we had our last row. That last row!—it was pretty lively that last row—but then so were most of the others. I doubt if any man and wife ever had more rows than we did in four years. And I don't see why we quarrelled either—I'm sure I'm good-natured enough. [*Pause.*] Snug little crib this. She always had good taste; I will say that for her. [*Rises, and stands by desk.*] There's the inkstand the mater gave her, and that's the writing-case the governor had made for her. [*Crosses to mantel-piece, and adjusts his cravat in mirror.*] Deuced dusty, these roads here in America. [*Moves up, and sees her photograph on mantel-piece.*] Her photo!"

[*As he takes it in his hand, Mrs. S. enters, and stands in doorway.*

Mrs. S. (*aside*): "What is he up to now? Oh, my portrait."

Mr. S. (*holding picture*): "I say, she hasn't been mourning for me, you know. She isn't fading away. She's positively improved. That's it—she's positively improved."

Mrs. S. (*aside*): "He's just as handsome as ever; and he looks as though he could be just as irritating."

Mr. S.: "She has filled out a bit, and it suits her. [*Putting back the photograph on mantel-piece, he catches sight of her in mirror, and is instantly confused.*] Oh, I say, she's been watching me. [*He goes up, pretending not to see her. He looks up finally and catches her eye. Moment of embarrass-*

3

ment. Hesitating.] I have — I — I have called—"

Mrs. S. (*sitting on sofa, calmly*) : " Take a chair, Mr. [*looking at card in her hand*]— Mr. Stanyhurst."

Mr. S. (*aside*): " That was one for me. Clever old girl. I thought she'd make it uncomfortable for me. [*Places chair, and sits. Aloud.*] Thank you. Standing makes a fellow feel so awkward."

Mrs. S.: " You have been abroad, I believe, Mr. [*glancing again at card*] — Mr. Stanyhurst."

Mr. S.: " I got back yesterday morning, on the *Etruria*, and so I—so I—" [*Confused.*

Mrs. S. (*after a pause*) : " And what gives me the honor of this visit?"

Mr. S.: " That's what I'm coming to— only you—you— Well, last night at the club I heard two fellows talking about our divorce case, you know—"   [*Pause.*

Mrs. S.: " Yes, I know."

Mr. S.: " They didn't know I was in New

York, and one of them said that Bull—that's my lawyer, you know—"

Mrs. S.: "Yes, I know that too."

Mr. S.: "He said my lawyer, Bull, had made some sort of disparaging remarks about you, you know."

Mrs. S.: "Yes, I know. And what then?"

Mr. S.: "What then? Well, you know, I didn't want you to think that I had anything to do with it—so I ran down here at once to tell you so."

Mrs. S.: "Oh, you need not have taken so much trouble for a little thing like that."

Mr. S.: "Of course I wouldn't let my lawyer say an insulting word to you."

Mrs. S.: "Of course not. That's a privilege you desire to reserve for yourself."

Mr. S.: "Come, now, I say — that isn't fair. That's one below the belt. Bull behaved like a brute, I dare say—"

Mrs. S.: "Like master, like man."

Mr. S.: "But I try to behave like a gentleman, I hope."

Mrs. S.: "No doubt you do your best."

Mr. S.: "And I come down here to tell you it's all a mistake, and I hadn't anything to do with it; and then you jump on me, as you Americans say."

Mrs. S.: "I'm by way of being irritated, as you English say. Your Bull lawyer was a brute—such a contrast to Mr. Hitchcock! You ought to have heard Mr. Hitchcock describe your infamous conduct to me. He almost made me cry when he told the judge how you had abandoned me, and refused to contribute to my support. Just as if I would ever ask you for a cent!"

Mr. S.: "Your lawyer seems to have been pitching into me."

Mrs. S.: "That's different."

Mr. S.: "Who is this Hitchcock fellow? I've met him somewhere, haven't I?"

Mrs. S.: "Mr. Hitchcock is my counsel. He has been kindness itself—and sympathy. He has the most exquisite manners, too. Of course he simply despises your little lawyer, but he treated him always with the most disdainful courtesy—except when that Bull insulted me, and then he talked back. It was so like you to hire a man of that sort. I could have smiled if I hadn't been so mad."

Mr. S.: "But I came here to tell you I—"

Mrs. S.: "Oh, I exonerate you, of course; I know you wouldn't have permitted it if you had been here."

Mr. S.: "Thanks, I'm sure."

Mrs. S.: "I was just writing to a friend [*taking letter out of pocket*], and I had told her that I didn't believe you were responsible."

Mr. S.: "That's really very good of you, you know. [*Pause.*] Oh, I say, if you've been writing like that, then I needn't have bothered to come down here."

Mrs. S.: "*If* I've been writing? So you are still as suspicious as ever. See for yourself!" [*Holding out the letter.*

Mr. S.: "Really—I—I—really—"

Mrs. S.: "See for yourself!"

Mr. S.: "I don't want to read your letters, you know, but if you insist—"

[*Reaching out hand for letter.*

Mrs. S. (*suddenly withdrawing letter*): "Perhaps you had better not read it, after all."

Mr. S.: "Just as you like."

Mrs. S. (*looking over the letter*): "There are other allusions to you, which — which it might be awkward for you to see."

[*Pocketing letter.*

Mr. S.: "It's all deuced awkward as it is, don't you know."

Mrs. S.: "It is indeed."

Mr. S.: "You see, until that judge makes up his mind, I don't know whether I'm a married man or not."

Mrs. S.: "Neither do I. I mean, I don't know whether I'm a married woman or not."

Mr. S.: "I'm like that fellow's coffin, you know—"

Mrs. S.: "That fellow's coffin? Oh, Mohammed's."

Mr. S. (*admiringly*): "You always knew such a lot! Yes, that's it—I'm like Mohammed's coffin—suspended between heaven and the other place, you know."

Mrs. S.: "The other place? Meaning me? Oh, thank you."

Mr. S. (*confused*): "Oh, I say!"

Mrs. S.: "That wasn't delicate, perhaps, but it was direct enough."

Mr. S.: "Come, now, I didn't mean that; you know I didn't mean that."

Mrs. S.: "It's no matter what you meant. I can judge of that only by what you say."

Mr. S. (*protesting*): "But—I—"

Mrs. S.: "After all, this suspense is ever so much worse for me than for you, for I don't even know what my name is."

Mr. S.: "I don't see that."

Mrs. S.: "You don't suppose that I shall keep your name, do you, when I cease to be your wife?"

Mr. S.: "My name's all right. Nobody's ever done anything to disgrace it yet."

Mrs. S. (*indignantly*): " You need not insinuate that I shall do so."

Mr. S. (*protesting*): " You do take one up
so sharp!"

Mrs. S.: "I am Mrs. Stanyhurst now, I
suppose, if the judge hasn't come to a decision yet. But when he does I shall take
my father's name again. I shall be Mrs.
Van Kortlandt."

Mr. S.: " You are not going to do that
really, are you?"

Mrs. S.: " Why not? You don't think
that I'm so proud of having married the
younger son of a lord that I'm going to hold
to the name after I've cast off the man?"

Mr. S.: "Cast off? I say, you mustn't
talk about me as if I was an old dressing-
gown."

Mrs. S.: "It's no matter what kind of ap-
parel you are. I'm not wrapped up in you
any longer. If I were only a widow, now!"

Mr. S.: " Oh, I say!"

Mrs. S.: " They are making such lovely

things in crape this year. But then you never had any consideration for me."

Mr. S.: "You wouldn't have me die just to leave you a widow?"

Mrs. S.: "Why not? When a man really loves a woman he is willing to die for her! Or at least he tells her so. It must be delightful for a woman to be a widow; she can do as she pleases, and make all the men do what she pleases. She is her own husband—and she has no wife."

Mr. S.: "If my widow were to remarry, I'd come back to worry her."

Mrs. S.: "Just as you did your wife? Precisely. As for me, since I can't be a widow, I must be the next best thing—divorced."

Mr. S.: "It is deuced awkward, of course."

Mrs. S.: "It is indeed deuced awkward —I mean, very awkward."

[*Pause. Clock on mantel-piece strikes five slowly.*

4

Mr. S. (*rising*): "Five o'clock. I must be going. I've got to get back to New York to-night."

[Mary *enters with kettle, puts it on stand on tea table before window, lights lamp, and carries table down and sets it before* Mrs. S. Mr. S. *awkwardly gets out of way of table.*

Mrs. S.: "Can't I offer you a cup of tea?"

Mr. S. (*astonished*): "Really you are very good, but—"

Mrs. S. (*lifting sugar-tongs*): "One lump or two?"

Mr. S.: "One, please."   [*Exit* Mary.

Mrs. S.: "Do you take cream?"

Mr. S.: "Come, now, you ought to know that—really, you know."

Mrs. S.: "No cream, then. But perhaps you would like a slice of lemon?"

Mr. S.: "No, thanks, no. I don't think I shall need any lemon."

[*Putting hat and cane on chair between*

piano and fireplace, and sitting on piano-stool.

Mrs. S. (*passing cup*) : " Five-o'clock tea always reminds me of marriage. You need two spoons, of course, and sooner or later they get into hot water."

Mr. S. (*taking cup and stirring it*) : " That's very good. That's very good indeed. But then I always said you were clever. [*Sipping tea, and getting scalded.*] The water was hot !"

[Mary *enters with plate of toasted crackers. She passes them to* Mr. S., *who takes one. Then she puts plate down on tea table, and exit.*

Mr. S. (*watching her off*) : " Pretty girl that."

Mrs. S. : " So you noticed it?"

Mr. S. : " I noticed that you never had any pretty girls like that when you and I—"

[Mrs. S. *looks at him.* Mr. S. *hesitates, and then stops, and drinks tea abruptly.*

Mrs. S.: "Don't judge others by yourself. *I'm* not jealous."

Mr. S. (*with mouth full*): "This toasted biscuit is really delicious."

Mrs. S.: "The biscuit? Oh, you mean the crackers? You English really ought to learn our language."

Mr. S.: "Your language? The English language? Well, I like that!"

Mrs. S.: "You would like it if you could only speak it as we do. When I hear our language maltreated by you English, I wish we Americans had kept our native Choctaw."

Mr. S.: "It isn't your native Choctaw, you know; you haven't any red-Indian blood in you."

Mrs. S.: "Haven't I? My grandmother was a Virginian, and I'm a direct descendant of Pocahontas—I'm her great-great-great-great-great-granddaughter."

Mr. S.: "Dear me!"

Mrs. S.: "Would you like me to do my ancestral scalp-dance for you?"

"HER PHOTO!"

Mr. S.: "It might be very good fun."

[*Rising and putting teacup on mantelpiece behind him.*

Mrs. S.: "I know that your family goes back to the time of the Black Prince, but I can trace mine back to a red princess."

Mr. S. (*negligently*): "Pocahontas was a nigger, wasn't she?"

Mrs. S.: "She was the daughter of King Powhatan!"

Mr. S. (*indifferently*): "I dare say."

Mrs. S.: "That's just like you English; you are abject before royalty in your own country, and yet you turn up your nose at our kings."

Mr. S. (*standing stiffly behind sofa*): "I didn't know you Americans had any kings."

Mrs. S.: "I've been thinking about these international marriages, as the society reporter calls them, and I've come to this conclusion, that if an American man marries an English woman, it's all right; but if an American woman marries an Englishman, it's all wrong. In the first case they get on splendidly, because the English woman is accustomed to be obedient, and the American man is in the habit of being attentive, and so both sides are satisfied. But in the second case there is slim chance of happiness, because the American woman is used to independence and to deference, and the Englishman is always waited on by all his women—mother, sisters, wife, daughters—just as if he were a Mormon."

Mr. S. (*protesting*): "Oh, I say!"

Mrs. S.: "There is not only incompatibility of temper; there is incompatibility of training. You, now, you—"

Mr. S.: "What about me, now?"

Mrs. S.: "You ought to have married some Lady Hildegarde Fitzplantagenet, who would have been happy to fetch your slippers for you and wait on you hand and foot, day and night. Instead you married Kitty Van Kortlandt — and we have both regretted it ever since."

Mr. S.: "Speak for yourself, Kitty [*she looks up*]—Mrs. Stanyhurst, I mean."

Mrs. S.: "It is too late for you to make me believe that you don't regret it now. No, you were not cut out for a husband, and—"

Mr. S. (*gallantly*): "If I thought any fellow had been cutting me out, I'd—"

Mrs. S. (*calmly*): "Well, what would you do?"

Mr. S. (*hesitating*): "I don't know. I—I—"

Mrs. S.: "What could you do? Nothing; that's what you could do. You see, I've had a good many hours of solitude in the past year, and I've spent some of them in analyzing your character."

Mr. S. (*energetically*): "I say, now, do you think that was fair?"

Mrs. S.: "Oh, I wasn't unjust to you; I gave you credit for your good qualities. You are not clever, for example, but you are not a fool either."

Mr. S.: "Thanks—thanks awfully."

Mrs. S.: "Your education is lamentable,

of course, but you know a lot about horses and dogs, and shooting and fishing, and sport of all kinds."

Mr. S.: "What else should I know?"

Mrs. S.: "What else indeed? Well, for one thing, you might know something about women — about the way a wife feels; you might have learned to look at life from her point of view, and to— [*Suddenly changing voice as* Mary *enters.*] It has been unusually warm for so late in September. Don't you think so?"

Mr. S. (*astonished*): "I? Don't I think? [*Seeing* Mary, *who is taking away tea things.*] Oh yes, I think so too. Of course. I agree with you."

[*Going up after* Mrs. S. Mary *exit with tray.*

Mrs. S. (*at window*): "Those dark clouds over there seem to threaten a storm soon. The equinoctial is due now."

[Mary *enters and takes table from before sofa and puts it before window.*

Mr. S.: "Shouldn't wonder if we had rain before night."

[*Looking over shoulder to see if* Mary *has gone.*

[Mary *looks at him and then at* Mrs. S , *and then exit.*

[Mrs. S. *stands looking at birds in conservatory bow-window.*

Mrs. S.: "And my birds are excited, too; that's another sign."

Mr. S. (*looking at cage with single eye-glass*): "What sort of birds?"

Mrs. S.: "Love-birds."

Mr. S.: "Funny little beggars."

Mrs. S. (*dryly*): "Their open affection for each other is rather absurd, isn't it? But they can't get out of the cage, you see; and, like many other couples, perhaps they are merely making the best of it, and pretend to affection while people are looking at them."

Mr. S. (*admiringly*): "You always did have a way of saying things."

Mrs. S.: "I've practised that speech before.

5

The last man I said it to was Mr. Hitchcock."

Mr. S.: "Hitchcock? Oh, he's your lawyer fellow? I remember now—you used to know him before we were married."

Mrs. S.: "He's a charming man. It's a pleasure to talk to him—he's so quick. He said that flirtation was more fun than marriage, just as a novel was more amusing than a history."

Mr. S.: "I don't see that that's so very clever."

Mrs. S.: "No? Then perhaps you won't approve of my retort that I didn't understand why marriage should be a bar to flirtation."

[Mr. S. *is about to protest, but is interrupted.*

Mrs. S. : "The privilege of flirting is guaranteed to every American woman by the Declaration of Independence ; it is the right to life, liberty, and the pursuit of happiness."

Mr. S.: "You Americans talk a great

deal about independence, but I remember
you had a chaperon the first time I met you
—at the Patriarchs', wasn't it?"

Mrs. S.: "It was at the Assembly. That
just shows how much you took notice of
me."

Mr. S.: "I did take notice of you. I remember what I said to the fellow who took
me to the dance."

Mrs. S.: "And pray what did you say?"

Mr. S.: "I said, 'That's a devilish pretty
girl, that Miss Van Kortlandt, and clever
too!' That's what I said."

[*Leaning back on desk.*

Mrs. S.: "Thank you. And what did he
say to that?"

Mr. S.: "What did he say? I remember
that too. He said: 'You just look out. Kitty Van Kortlandt is a terrible flirt!' That's
what he said."

Mrs. S.: "The idea! As if I ever flirted!"

Mr. S.: "You didn't flirt with me, I know
that. You wouldn't even dance with me."

Mrs. S.: "You know you dance like a bear."

Mr. S.: "Come, now—"

Mrs. S.: "You English don't begin to know anything about dancing. I can't think what they teach you in your schools. Do you remember the first time you tried 'Dancing in the Barn?' [*Laughing, and crossing to piano, and playing the tune while talking over her shoulder to* Mr. S., *who has followed her across.*] It was here in Newport, at the De Ruyters', five years ago, when they gave their first ball at their new cottage on the Cliffs."

Mr. S.: "You have such queer dances here, you know."

Mrs. S. (*still playing*): "We never had a queerer dancer than you were when I tried to show you 'Dancing in the Barn.' You looked so absurd."

Mr. S.: "Did I, though?"

Mrs. S.: "You did indeed. So at last I took pity on you, and I gave up the dance, and we went out on the piazza."

Mr. S.: "Yes. I liked that better."

Mrs. S. (*still playing*): "So did I."

Mr. S.: "That was the first time you had been polite to me, don't you know. Before that you were always offish. I never knew how to take you."

Mrs. S.: "Perhaps I didn't intend to let you take me at all."

Mr. S.: "I know I didn't think I'd ever let any American girl take me."

Mrs. S. (*still playing, but more slowly, and "Dancing in the Barn" has changed into a waltz of Chopin's*): "You don't suppose I had intended to marry an Englishman, do you? I don't know how I ever came to do it. It must have been the music and the moonlight—I remember there was a heavenly moon that evening."

Mr. S.: "Was there? I don't know. But I remember you looked devilish pretty."

Mrs. S.: "Did I?"

[*Turning on piano-stool and facing him.*

Mr. S.: "You did. And I remember I

said to myself: 'I'll risk it. I don't know whether she'll have me, but I'll risk it.' And I asked you to marry me."

Mrs. S.: "And do you remember what I said?"

Mr. S.: "You said you wouldn't. But you looked so charming and so tantalizing— I don't know how it was, but I kissed you."

Mrs. S.: "Don't you think that it was very ungentlemanly to kiss a lady who had just refused to marry you?"

Mr. S.: "I'm not so sure about that, you know. You let me, you know."

Mrs. S.: "There wasn't anything else for me to do. You were a great big hulking man, and I was only a girl."

Mr. S.: "You made me fetch and carry for you that winter; I remember that well enough. You led me a pretty dance, I can tell you."

Mrs. S. (*sadly*): "A girl can be engaged only once, and if she does not have a good time then, when is she to have it?"

Mr. S.: "I dare say you had a good time, as you call it. I know I didn't. I don't like going about to balls and parties night after night, and seeing the girl I'm going to marry dancing with a parcel of fellows who—"

Mrs. S.: "But you know you dance so badly. I simply couldn't dance with you. I shouldn't have had a ball dress to my back."

Mr. S.: "I was glad when the winter was over and we were married."

Mrs. S.: "At Grace Church, by the Bishop, on a beautiful spring morning. [*Facing piano again, and playing the " Wedding March " of "Lohengrin" gently.*] I'm sure it must have been a lovely wedding. The church was crowded, and all my friends were there in their spring bonnets. The music was heavenly—and there are people who say they don't like Wagner!" [*Pause.*

Mr. S. (*watching her; aside*): "She's handsomer than ever. She didn't look better on her wedding-day than she does now. I wonder if— [*Pause.*] By Jove, I will!"

[*Goes to extreme end of piano, so that he
faces her.*

[Mrs. S. *continues playing softly, con-
scious that he is gazing at her; she
changes time of music, plays louder
and more brilliantly, and then stops
abruptly.*

Mrs. S. (*with a return of her former sharp
manner*): "A divorce isn't as romantic as a
wedding, is it? Nor as picturesque. There
isn't half enough ceremony about a divorce.
There's no music, no veil, no flowers, no
bridemaids, no Bishop. They'll never make
divorce really popular with the women till
it is as spectacular as a wedding, with ushers,
and best men, and pretty girls, and cake—
cake to take home in a box, so that every
woman can dream of the man she is some
day to be divorced from."

Mr. S.: "Oh, I say, now, that's too bad,
really."

Mrs. S.: "And of course there would have
to be something to correspond with the

honey - moon and the wedding trip. Perhaps the happy pair who had just been divorced would go on a little journey around the world, one east and one west, with an understanding that they should pass each other in the middle of the Pacific Ocean."

Mr. S.: "When we were married we went home, you know."

Mrs. S.: "It was home for you, of course, but it was exile for me."

Mr. S. (*stifly*): "My people were good to you, weren't they? The governor thought you were no end of fun."

Mrs. S.: "Yes; I received the welcome of a professional humorist."

Mr. S.: "The mater liked you. You can't deny that, can you?"

Mrs. S.: "I think she did—in her way. The first time we met she told me she was so glad you had a wife to keep you out of mischief."

Mr. S. (*exultingly*): "She never would have

said that if she hadn't cottoned to you from the start, would she?"

Mrs. S.: "And she said she was glad to find I had so little Yankee twang—as if we were Yankees in New York! And she has an English accent of her own as thick as a London fog. You could cut it with a knife [*imitating*], don't you know."

Mr. S. (*stiffly again*): "I think all my people were very civil to you."

Mrs. S. (*bitterly*): "Yes, as war is sometimes civil, and then the wounds rankle longest."

Mr. S.: "The governor was nice to you—nicer than he is to me half the time. And the mater—"

Mrs. S. (*impatiently*): "No doubt the governor and the mater, as you call them, meant to be nice, as you say. They were as nice as they knew how. [*Sitting on sofa.*] But, oh, how hard it was to be in the same house with such simple folks! I'm complicated, I am, and intricate; I'm modern and nineteenth century. And your father and mother are simple beyond belief, simple with a pre-historic simplicity — so simple that when I saw them go out for a walk together, I was always expecting that the robins would come and cover them up with leaves."

Mr. S.: "You are deuced hard on my people. Now I never say anything about yours."

Mrs. S.: "How can you? You had an un-fair advantage when we married. I'm an orphan."

Mr. S. (*doubtfully*): "There's your brother, you know."

Mrs. S. (*suddenly*): "I know what you were going to say. Well, it's true, he does drink, sometimes—but then he is frequently sober."

Mr. S.: "I wasn't going to say it. I don't care if he gets as drunk as a lord. That might happen to any fellow, you know. After the second bottle, wine goes to my head sometimes."

Mrs. S.: "It's no news that nature abhors a vacuum."

Mr. S.: "I don't see anything funny in that."

Mrs. S. (*laughing*): "Don't you? Well, perhaps it was unfair. Don't mind my being sharp with you to-day. There's a storm coming, and my nerves are unstrung."

Mr. S. (*leaning over the back of the sofa*): "Do you remember that storm we had crossing the Channel when we went over to the continent?"

Mrs. S. (*shuddering*): "Shall I ever forget it? I thought I should never see land again. But you—I will say that for you—you were not a bit frightened."

Mr. S. (*laughing lightly*): "Frightened? There was only a capful of wind."

Mrs. S.: "It ruffled the feathers in my cap, I can tell you; and I was glad to get my foot on shore again. I did enjoy my first dinner in Paris: you hadn't any idea where Worth's was, but you knew all the good restaurants."

Mr. S.: "They give you filthy things to eat in Paris, if you don't know where to go."

Mrs. S.: "Yes, we had a good time in Paris then."

Mr. S.: "And in Switzerland."

Mrs. S.: "Yes, we had a good time in Switzerland too."

Mr. S.: "It was very jolly, Paris and Switzerland, and all that. We were happy then, weren't we?"

Mrs. S.: "I suppose so."

Mr. S. (*suddenly*): "That's what I say! Well, now, why shouldn't we be happy again? You know I always loved you."

Mrs. S.: "I used to think so."

Mr. S.: "Think so again, can't you?"

Mrs. S.: "I don't know."

Mr. S.: "And you loved me then, when we were on our honey-moon and wedding trip, and all that, you know. Is all that love gone? Don't you love me at all now? [*Pause.*] You don't hate me, do you? You say sharp things to me, but I don't mind that, you know. I've got a tough hide of my own, and I don't mind it. Besides, I know you don't mean anything by it. Now come, let's have a fresh start, and see if we can't get off all together this time. It's odds we make a better match of it now than we did at the first meeting. We got along first rate in Paris and Switzerland. I've got to go to San Francisco to-morrow. Come with me."

Mrs. S.: "Oh, I can't."

Mr. S.: "Come with me, and we'll have a second wedding trip and honey-moon and all that. It'll be better than the first time of asking. Come."

Mrs. S.: "I can't, I can't. Oh, what would people say?"

Mr. S.: "Damn people! Who cares what they say? They say too much always. It's all right for husband and wife to go off travelling together, isn't it? And you are my wife, aren't you, Kitty?"

Mrs. S.: "Am I? Am I *now?* Perhaps

the judge has made up his mind by this time."

Mr. S.: "The divorce? I forgot about the divorce! We can stop the divorce, can't we?"

Mrs. S. (*thoughtfully*): "I suppose so. [*Rising and facing him.*] So you think you are in love with me still? I doubt it. I don't believe it. It's all a delusion on your part. And I'm a delusion too."

Mr. S. (*coming forward to her*): "I'd like to hug that delusion. [*Putting his arm about her.*] Say you will withdraw the suit."

Mrs. S. (*escaping from him*): "I can't, I can't—but you may, if you insist."

Mr. S. (*following her*): "It isn't my suit, you know. I'm not going to court to compel you to support me, am I?"

Mrs. S.: "Of course that was only an excuse."

Mr. S.: "It isn't a good excuse, now. I'm ready to support you."

[*With his arm about her again.*

Mrs. S.: "But if you did take me off to San Francisco, the judge might divorce us while we were on our second honey-moon."

Mr. S.: "That's what I say, don't you know. You must withdraw the suit."

Mrs. S.: "How can I?"

[*Messenger-boy is seen through windows. He stands before the door, and rings bell.*

Mrs. S. (*starting*): "What's that? [*With hand to heart.*] It's a messenger-boy! He has a telegram! Perhaps the judge has made up his mind."

Mr. S.: "Perhaps he has."

Mrs. S.: "I'm certain it's the decision—absolutely certain. And Mr. Hitchcock said he would telegraph me at once."

[*Door opens, and messenger-boy disappears in house.*

Mrs. S.: "I know now how a person feels when he is waiting for the verdict."

Mr. S.: "It is awkward, isn't it?—deuced

awkward. But I shall be glad to know whether we are man and wife or not."

[Mary *enters, with telegram on a salver*.

Mary: "A telegram for you, ma'am."

Mrs. S. (*taking it*): "I don't dare to know my fate." [Mary *exit*.

Mr. S.: "Don't hesitate. You might as well get it over as soon as you can. Have your tooth out at once if it aches. I always do."

Mrs. S. (*tears open envelope, reads telegram, and drops her arm*): "So that is settled."

Mr. S.: "Is there a decision?"

Mrs. S.: "Yes."

[*Holding out the telegram to him*.

Mr. S. (*taking it*): "Let's see. Really, I'm a bit nervous myself. [*Reads*.] 'Court granted your application this afternoon. You are again a free woman. [*Stops and looks at* Mrs. S.] I congratulate you on being separated from the brute who has made you so miserable. Will bring down papers to-morrow. Richard Hitchcock.'"

7

Mrs. S. (*snatching telegram*): "I didn't mean you to read it all."

Mr. S. (*indignantly*): "He didn't mean me to read it either. You can let me go, can't you? Now that Hitchcock has done what you wanted him to do. I knew he'd do anything for you!"

Mrs. S. (*turning suddenly, with change of manner*): "What do you mean by that?"

Mr. S. (*shrinking back a little*): "He's a friend of yours, isn't he?"

Mrs. S. (*insisting, and with rising temper*): "That isn't what you mean. You know it isn't!"

Mr. S.: "Come, now, don't be so sharp on a fellow—don't. I meant what I said, didn't I? He's your lawyer, this Hitchcock, isn't he? And he's got to do what you tell him."

Mrs. S.: "But that isn't all you meant. You forget that I know your ways of old."

Mr. S.: "I say, now, don't let's dig up old bones."

Mrs. S.: "And you said it in time, fortunately. I might have been fool enough to listen to you again. But I'm not going to make myself the victim of your absurd suspicions a second time."

Mr. S.: "Suspicions?"

Mrs. S.: "I'm not going to suffer again from your ridiculous jealousy."

Mr. S.: "Jealousy? I say, now, this isn't a joke!"

Mrs. S. (*coming up close and looking him in the eye*): "Do you dare to tell me that you did not intend to insinuate that I had been flirting with Mr. Hitchcock?"

Mr. S. (*taken aback*): "I? I suggest that? Nothing of the sort, I assure you."

Mrs. S. (*turning away from him*): "Don't be a hypocrite too—don't! Don't try to sneak out of it. To be suspicious and jealous is bad enough, but you might at least be frank about it."

Mr. S.: "Oh, I say, this is really too bad, you know. I didn't say anything about this Hitchcock; I didn't mean to insinuate anything; I wasn't even thinking about his attentions to you. I wasn't indeed. [*Pause.*] Come to think of it, though, he took your case up eagerly, I'm told, and I know he pitched into me in court. He pitched in pretty strong, too—didn't he?"

Mrs. S.: "He had to tell the truth about you—didn't he?"

Mr. S.: "I suppose the fellow was glad of a chance to get even with me. He knew you before you were married, and I doubt he has ever forgiven me for cutting him out."

Mrs. S.: "There you go again! That's the way you always are. You object now to the friends of my childhood. I wonder what next. I suppose you won't want me to see my own brother soon!"

Mr. S. (*laughing harshly*): "I don't mind your seeing him, but I shouldn't grieve if I never laid eyes on him again."

Mrs. S.: "That's unworthy of you. Oh, I know what you are going to say."

Mr. S.: "I'm not going to say anything."

Mrs. S.: "You are going to say that my brother has called on you at the office and at the club, perhaps a little flushed with wine."

Mr. S.: "Flushed with wine? He couldn't stand straight. He hung around the neck of the club porter."

Mrs. S.: "I've no doubt it is true—although of course you exaggerate; but it isn't nice of you to say it."

Mr. S.: "I didn't say it, did I?"

Mrs. S.: "I've never accused your father or your mother of drinking."

Mr. S.: "Come, now, I say—"

Mrs. S. (*dropping in chair, and wiping eyes with handkerchief*): "Before we had been married a month, I saw you didn't understand me."

Mr. S. (*impatiently walking up and down*): "I don't understand you now, that's clear."

Mrs. S.: "I had been writing to a friend this very afternoon [*taking letter out of pocket*], and I told her you had always been a brute to me."

Mr. S.: "Oh, you told her that, did you?"

Mrs. S.: "Do you doubt me again? [*Holding out letter.*] See for yourself."

Mr. S.: "Thanks, but I don't care to see for myself."

Mrs. S.: "I told her there was not merely a personal disagreement between us; there was also a total international incompatibility. No Englishman could make an American woman happy; and that I never expected to set eyes on you again, and that I didn't want to. [*Looking over letter.*] I thought I wrote her that. But that must have been in a letter to somebody else."

[*Putting letter in pocket.*

Mr. S. (*sharply*): "If there are two women you've been telling you don't want to see me again, there's no use my stopping here any longer."

Mrs. S.: "Certainly not."

Mr. S. (*taking hat and gloves*): "I'm going

to San Francisco to-morrow. It's odds I never see you again, you know."

Mrs. S.: " True. You will probably never see me again. Well, I wish you a pleasant journey, Mr. Stanyhurst."

Mr. S.: "And I wish you a good-after-noon, Mrs. Van Kortlandt."

Mrs. S. (*mechanically repeating*) : "Mrs. Van Kortlandt ?"

> [Mr. S. *bows automatically, but she does not look at him as he leaves the room.*
>
> [Mrs. S. *stands silent as he is seen passing the windows. As he goes out of sight she glances up quickly.*

V

[*Mrs. S. suddenly takes the letter from her pocket, and goes to the desk.*

Mrs. S. (*writing*): " ' P.S.—The decision has just been rendered, and I'm a single woman again.   Congratulate me.' "

[*She puts the letter in the envelope, seals it, leaves it on the desk as she rises, crosses to sofa, turns and looks up at window, and then drops on sofa, burying her face in her handkerchief. Mary enters, followed by the messenger-boy.*

Mary: "Is there any answer to that telegram, ma'am?   The boy is waiting."

Mrs. S. (*automatically*): "The boy is waiting.   [*Suddenly springing to her feet.*]   Where is the boy?"

Boy: "I'm here."

Mrs. S. (*seizing boy and rushing him to the window, which she throws open*): "Boy, do you see that gentleman there? The one walking so fast?"

Boy (*out on piazza*): "The one with the cane and the dicer? I see him."

Mrs. S.: "Then run after him quick and tell him to come back—"

Boy: "All right."   [*Exit.*

Mrs. S. (*half out on piazza*): "Tell him I've changed my mind! Tell him there was something I forgot to say to him. Tell him— Oh, he can tell him what he likes, so long as he brings him back. [*Pause.*] The boy has caught him. [*Pause.*] He's coming! [*Pause. Then suddenly she leaves window and goes to sofa, standing behind it, with her back to the window.*] And what shall I say to him when he comes?"   [*Pause.*

Boy (*at window*): "Here he is. I got him easy."

Mr. S. (*at window*): "Kitty! [*Stepping inside.*] Did you send for me?"

8

Mrs. S.: "No. [*Looking around.*] Oh, is that you?"

Mr. S.: "You sent for me. Did you want to ask me something?"

Mrs. S.: "Did I? Yes; I wanted to ask you how long it will take us to go to San Francisco."

And so the curtain falls, with Mr. Stanyhurst's arm about Mrs. Stanyhurst, and with Mary and the messenger-boy looking at them wonderingly.

THE END.

www.ingramcontent.com/pod-product-compliance
Lightning Source LLC
Chambersburg PA
CBHW022155020726
47496CB00008B/2724